BY LAURA E. RICHARDS

JIGGLE JOGGLE JEE!

PICTURES BY
SAM WILLIAMS

Greenwillow Books
An Imprint of HarperCollinsPublishers

What does
the train say?

Jiggle joggle,
jiggle joggle,
jiggle joggle

What does
the train say?

Jiggle joggle

jee!

Will the little baby go Riding with the locomo?

Loky moky poky stoky

smoky choky chee!

Ting! Ting! The bells ring.

Jiggle joggle, jiggle joggle

Ting! Ting! The bells ring.

Jiggle joggle jee!

Ring for joy
because we go

Riding

with the locomo,

Look! How the trees run.

jiggle joggle,

jiggle joggle

Each chasing
t'other one.

Jiggle joggle jee!

Are they running for to go
Riding with the locomo?

Loky moky
poky stoky . . .

smoky choky

Over the hills now,

Jiggle joggle,

jiggle joggle

Down through the vale below.

Jiggle
joggle
jee!

All the cows
and horses run,
Crying, "Won't you
take us on?

Loky moky poky

So, so, the miles go,

Jiggle joggle, jiggle joggle

Now it's fast . . .

and now it's slow.

Jiggle joggle
jee!

When we're at
our journey's end,
Say good-bye
to snorting friend.

Loky moky poky stoky
smoky choky chee!

To Susan, Ava, and Virginia . . .
Thank you, thank you, thank you!
—S. W.

The poem in this book, originally titled "The Baby Goes to Boston," was written by Laura E. Richards
in the early 1900s. It appears under that title in *Tirra Lirra: Rhymes Old and New* by Laura E. Richards,
published by Little, Brown and Company (Copyright, 1902, 1906, by Dana Estes and Company; Copyright,
1930, 1932, 1934, by Laura E. Richards; Copyright, 1955, by Little, Brown and Company). Reprinted
by permission of Little, Brown and Company.

Jiggle Joggle Jee!
Illustrations © 2001 by Sam Williams
All rights reserved. Printed in Singapore by Tien Wah Press.
www.harperchildrens.com

Pencil and watercolors were used for the full-color art.
The text type is Goudy Modern.

Library of Congress Cataloging-in-Publication Data
Richards, Laura Elizabeth Howe, 1850-1943.
Jiggle joggle jee! / by Laura E. Richards; illustrated by Sam Williams.
p. cm.
"Greenwillow Books."
Summary: Baby goes for a rollicking ride
on a jiggling, joggling locomotive.
ISBN 0-688-17832-4 (trade). ISBN 0-688-17833-2 (lib. bdg.)
[1. Railroads—Trains—Fiction. 2. Babies—Fiction.
3. Stories in rhyme.] I. Williams, Sam, ill.
II. Title. PZ8.3.R392 Ji 2001 [E]—dc21 00-057306

1 2 3 4 5 6 7 8 9 10 First Edition